Disco Club
of
Blood

Lee J. Minter

Top Circle Publishing

Published by Top Circle Publishing.

ISBN: 978-1-7340930-4-9 (e)
ISBN: 978-1-7340930-5-6 (sc)

This story is dedicated to all of those
who love the unknown and seek the truth.

Contents

Prologue 7

Chapter One 13

Chapter Two 19

Chapter Three 21

Chapter Four 39

Chapter Five 45

Chapter Six 51

Chapter Seven 57

Chapter Eight 61

Chapter Nine 65

Chapter Ten 71

Chapter Eleven 75

Epilogue 81

Bonus Excerpt: *Midnight Rain* 87

Also by the Author 94

Prologue

The city of Pontiac had now fallen on hard times when its main factory and job producer General Motors finally shut its doors, and thousands of jobs that Pontiac's residents held were now gone. First, the Pontiac Silverdome was the home to major sports teams, The Detroit Lions, Pistons, and Detroit Mechanix. It had also served as a venue for concerts and motocross that had bit the dust after Its retractable roof problems. Other building maintenance issues followed and became too expensive to fix and maintain by its owners.

What was now left in the aftermath of all of this was a city on the verge of economic bankruptcy and vast unemployment. In the place of that long-gone prosperity came a proliferation of drugs and other social malfeasances that were more than happy to take its place.

Despite its social and economic ills, its young people still wanted to party inside and outside of the city that was now trying to re-establish itself as a venue with thriving nightclubs and a vibrant social scene.

One of those places to go and party was an old Cathedral building, formerly a church located on Saginaw Street in Pontiac, Michigan. Decommissioned and sold by owners First Church Of Pontiac three years ago and converted into a nightclub called Tentacles, a popular hot spot and hangout for young adults on the weekends.

In contrast, its closest neighbor across the street was a recovery and rehabilitation center for men, women, and children addicted or homeless. First Steps to Recovery and Hope. Which also happens to be owned, connected, and run by the First Church Of Pontiac.

Tentacles was a spacious nightclub, thirty thousand square feet with three floors and a sanctuary with a balcony that seated up to six hundred and fifty people. That included an overflow space for an additional; one hundred people and a bar situated on each floor for thirsty patrons who wanted to cool their palettes with something wet after twerking, bumping, and grinding. The main floor was house music, techno, and disco. The second floor was "urban music," and the third floor was reserved for hip hop.

Although there were three other nightspots close by in Pontiac, none of them had the allure Tentacles did on the young college crowd on the weekends and "Thirsty Thursdays," as the club's promoter billed that day before the weekend for extra revenue. The club's consistent advertising on the local radio stations and one of the local stations broadcasting live from the club on weekends also help to hype up its reputation even more as the place to party and be on the weekends. That and the scantily clad young women even on the colder nights in Pontiac, Michigan. That attracted the young studs with dreams of scoring a one-night stand or maybe some mystery head from one of what they called bobbleheads in one of the club's numerous skanky bathrooms. Now, if they wanted to be more discreet inside their ride outside in the building's sixty car capacity parking lot, which every frequent flyer to the club knew that if you did not get to the club by at least 10:00 pm, the small lot for a building that size would be fill up to capacity, and you would have to use the adjacent overflow lot across the street at the rehab center that cost you five dollars to park, which most of the young crowd did not want to pay because it was cutting into their weed and beer money.

Community rumors now flowed that the church was now cursed after they had converted to a nightclub. Talk that the building was a haven for demonic activity and haunted. All of these subjective rumors did nothing, though, to curtail its customers from patronizing its new establishment. In fact, it seemed to have just the opposite effect and made it an even more popular destination and hangout spot due to its association with these creepy allegations. The church turned nightclub had a giant "Kraken-like" Squid adorning its outside brick wall with its appendages stretched out widely with Tentacles' name in colorful letters above it. This unofficial mascot was also painted and illustrated over the entrance in another position which gave it the appearance of it staring down at the patrons with outstretched and welcoming arms (tentacles) as they entered the nightspot.

* * *

Javon brushed the waves in his hair and sipped from a rolling rock beer he held in the other as he stood in front of the bathroom mirror with a shower towel wrapped around his waist. "Hey roomies, where are we hanging out tonight?' he yelled out at his two best friends Marty and Scott, engaged in the video game "Call Of Duty" on a nearby sofa.

Scott took a toke on the blunt between his fingers. "Man, I heard about this new place called Tentacles; we should check it out," he said as he exhaled out the vapors.

"Is that right? Where is it at?" Javon asked.

"Pontiac," Scott answered. "Goddammit, he just got me," he yelled out in frustration, referring to just being killed in the game.

"Fella's, the party is up here; what are we fucking around down there for?" Marty said.

"Man, I am tired of these stuck-up bitches around here. I just want to meet some down-to-earth girls for a change," Javon replied as he finished drying himself off with the towel.

"You mean some girls that are dumber than you," Marty said sarcastically, grinning.

"Fuck you, man," Javon said, laughing.

Javon walked out of the bathroom towards Scott and Marty with the towel still wrapped around his lean and muscular body.

"Let me hit that blunt," he said to Scott.

"Why don't you put some clothes on your ass and stop walking around here butt ass naked," Scott said as he passed Javon the joint.

Javon took a long drag of the blunt himself and then

passed it back to Scott. "Why? Your Mother never complains," he shot back smiling.

Scott laughed. "Really, she said you came up short last night, Peewee."

Marty burst out laughing, spitting out some of his beer. "That's cold. He got you there, bro."

"Man, whatever," Javon said, walking back towards the bathroom.

"Don't get mad, homie, cuz you got your junk posted all over social media; we warned you about dating that crazy-ass Juanita from that sorority," Marty said.

"Yeah, that was cold, but I did do her dirty by sleeping with her cousin."

"Which one was better?" Marty asked.

Javon takes another swig of his beer and smiles. "Their Aunt!" he answers.

Marty and Scott both exploded in laughter. "Homie, you're out cold," Marty said, still chuckling.

Javon stepped back out of the bathroom, this time with a tank top on and a pair of lounge pants. He walked over to their fridge, grabbed three *Rolling Rock* beers out of it, and popped the tops off all three. "So what's the game plan fella's for tonight?" he asked as he passed his boys off the other two bottles.

"Fucking Tentacles!" Marty shouted out enthusiastically as they all raised their cheap green bottles of beers in a mutual toast of agreement.

Chapter One

Farmington Hills, Michigan. "I see you, girl, you going to have those nigga's thirsting tonight," Gabriella said to her friend Crystal, who had FaceTime her to show herself off in a new dress that she was wearing for their girls night out that evening.

Crystal twirled back and forth, smiling, flipping her hair up as she held her iPhone out in front of her on a selfie stick. The hot pink dress did indeed complement her svelte hourglass figure.

"Crystal, you better have the right hoe shoes to go with that dress, girl."

"You know it," she answered as she put the camera on her diamond and studded encrusted heels. "Oh my god bitch I hate you. Now I gotta go dig deep in my closet tonight," Gabriella said with envy.

"I love you too, Gabby," Crystal said, laughing.

"Hold on, I got an incoming call," she said.

"Hey Ms. Thing, it looks like you are ready to party," Pepper said, smiling as Crystal three-way her on FaceTime.

Crystal pumped her hands in the air, smiling. "Girl, you know it."

"Hey Pepper, what's up?" Gabriella said as Pepper entered the video chat.

"Hey Gabby, I am babysitting my little brother Juno until my parents get back."

"Say hello, to my bitches - Crystal and Gabby," Pepper said as she brought her cute little five-year-old little brother Juno onto the chat. "Hey bitches," he said in a small voice, causing them all to burst out in laughter.

"Oh my god, no, he didn't," said Gabriella with her hand over her mouth.

"Juno, bad word, do not use that word," Crystal said. "Okay," Juno replied.

"Are you going to tell Mommy?" he asked.

"No, I am not going to tell her shit, now go play," Pepper said.

"Ooooooo – you said shit! That's a bad word," he said.

"Boy, I am grown, I am allowed to curse," his sister responded, smacking her lips.

"No, you're not, you're a child like me," he said.

"You little smart ass, I said go play," Pepper said, frowning her face up, causing her little brother to run off.

"Oh, he is so freaking adorable," Gabriella gushed.

"Please, girl, do not let his cute face fool you all. He's Chucky in disguise; that's why I hide all the damn kitchen knives in the house," Pepper said.

"For real?" Crystal asked.

"Naw, I am just fucking with y'all," Pepper answers. "He's more like Damien 3.0," she said, laughing.

"Pepper, you off the chain girl," Gabriella said, grinning.

"Hey guys, I gotta go. I think I hear my parents pulling up," Crystal said.

"Okay, Pepper, don't stand us up tonight," Crystal said.

"No way, I've been holed up in this house for a week, and it's time to get out and get some fresh air," she said.

"And some fresh dickkkkkk," Gabby shouted out.

"Girl, you so nasty, bye," Crystal said, laughing.

" Oh, by the way, before I let you go, where are we hanging out tonight? So that I can let my parents know," asked Pepper.

"Pepper, are you serious? You're still telling your parents your every freaking move?" Crystal asked, making Pepper feel instantly guilty and immature.

"No, that's not it at all," she answered back defensively.

"Good, then be ready by 9:00 pm to roll out," Crystal said. Not accustomed to hearing the word no, in her shelter and privilege world that her parents' money and influence provided for her lifestyle, she flaunted on Facebook and Twitter that had amassed Crystal a vast social media following in return.

"Bitch," Pepper said underneath her breath as she disconnected from the call.

"Dad and Mommy back!" she heard her little brother Juno scream out excitedly downstairs.

"I am coming," Pepper yelled back down to her little brother before heading downstairs to greet her parents as she thought up a lie to tell them regarding where she would be hanging out tonight. And although she hated lying to her parents, she hated losing face and looking weak in her friend Crystal's eyes even more.

In fact, in many ways, she wished she could be more like Crystal, who seemed able to speak her mind no matter the consequences and who she was interacting with socially. And if you were her friend and someone crossed you, Crystal was always the first to speak up and come to your defense fiercely. On the contrary, her other friend Gabriella was more of a laid-back go-with-the-flow person. But at the same time very observative and intelligent in her own right and did not take any shit off anybody either, including their friend Crystal, something Pepper wished she could do more often, instead of being so passive-aggressive.

"Hey guys," Pepper said, greeting her parents as they entered the house.

"Hey honey, thanks for watching your little brother. By the way, how was he?" her father asked.

Pepper looked at Juno and smiled. "Like a little angel," she said, smiling. Juno stuck his thumbs in his ears, wiggling his fingers while making a funny face at his big sister as he stood behind their father's leg for cover and protection.

"Archangel," Pepper truthfully thought, frowning quickly before bringing her face back into a fake smile.

"How was that new Chinese restaurant?" Pepper asked.

"Dear, don't ask," her mom said as she removed her heels.

"Yeah, I have never seen *egg foo young* made like Quiche," her father answered.

"Yes, and that fried rice was horrendous; it tasted as if they recycled it off another guest's plate," her mom added.

"Gross," Pepper said, sticking her tongue out as well.

"You should Yelp them," Pepper said.

"Yelp, pretty damn nasty," her father quipped, causing her to laugh.

"That's not what I meant, dad," Pepper said.

"I am still hungry; let's order a pizza and put a good movie on," her mom suggested.

"Pizza!" Juno yelled out! Jumping up and down ecstatically.

"That sounds good, Mom, but I already made plans to hang out with Crystal and Gabby tonight."

"Dear, it's okay. Where are you going, and what time will you be back?" her mom asked.

Shit! Pepper thought. Here come the lies.

Chapter Two

The Lexus pulled up in front of Pepper's house with horns honking as its two occupants giggled. "Tell Crystal to lay off the horn she is going to wake up the whole damn neighborhood!" her father said, annoyed.

"Dad, it's only nine o'clock," Pepper said.

"The only thing that goes to bed that early is old people and puppies," she said sarcastically.

"Funny," her father said as he bit into his slice of pizza.

"Be safe, baby," her mother said, kissing her on the cheek.

"I will love you," Pepper said.

Pepper looked over at her dad with that look on his face, tapping his watch. " Don't forget Pepper," he said.

"I gotta go. Love you too, dad," she said.

As he watched his daughter leave, he shook his head sideways in disapproval. "That kid is going to be the death of us," he said.

"Don't be a grouch. She's young; let her have some fun," her mom said, coming to her daughter's defense.

"You do remember what it was like when you were younger, don't you?" his wife asked.

"Nope, my youth went away with my hair, the birth

of our second child, and baby shark," he replied. As he went to his bay window and watched his daughter and her friends pull off. He recognized Crystal's car, which brought him some relief. Maybe he was too strict on Pepper, he thought. After all, she had never done anything not to warrant his and her mother's complete trust. Maybe he would loosen the reins. He felt, after all, Pepper would soon be turning eighteen years old next month.

"Bowling?" he said to his wife, sitting on the sofa with their son between them watching an animated movie.

"Yes, Shady Green Oaks Bowling Alley, " answered his wife. About where Pepper told them she would be hanging out tonight with her girlfriends.

"Bowling outfits sure have changed since I was a kid," he said.

"Yes, dear, this ain't "Happy Days no more," his wife shot back condescendingly.

He looked down at their son Juno ruffling his hair as he ate his pizza.

"Don't grow up too quick, kid," he said.

"I won't," his son surprisingly replied.

Chapter Three

Tentacles had three deejays providing the music for Friday's night party. But the headliner was Deejay Reptile, a deejay that wore a human-like lizard face mask with a tail included. The club owners thought his act was a bit over the top, but his presence and abilities seemed to bring in the crowds and the money. Therefore, if his fantasy was to be a lizard that spins turntables and mixes music, more power to him, they thought as long as the cash flowed in behind his eccentric deejay persona. The other two deejays were residents and knew the music scene quite well at the club and how to keep the party going until 2:00 am—closing time.

* * *

The crowd was already starting to gather and build up outside the club in the cold November weather. That did not stop the young women from wearing their skimpiest and tightest outfits with high heels included. Most of them had not dressed for the weather and were only concerned about how cute they would look amongst their friends in their latest and hip outfits. The cheap rum and vodka flowing through their bloodstream made some oblivious to just how chilly the November weather was, while others felt the cold bite of the wind and could not wait to get inside, to get warm, and get drunk.

"Man, this joint is off the hook!" Javon said excitedly as he and his friends made their way towards the club's front doors as they eyeballed the groups of young women headed in the same direction as them.

"The female to male ratio must be at least 10 to 1, he added."

"I don't know about that, but so far, not bad," Scott said, as an attractive young lady met eyes with him and smiled.

"You tripping roomie, I saw that eye play you just got," Javon said, grinning.

"Don't hate the player, hate the game," Scott said, puffing his shirt out, smiling.

Javon laughed. "See, I taught him well," he said to their friend Marty who laughed as well.

"Man, check out that eye candy over there," he said, pointing to the three girls ahead of them in the line. One of the young women in the group looked over at them and smiled.

"Shit! It's cold as hell out here," Marty said, clenching his teeth together.

"Hey, I got an idea. Let's go over there and pretend we are with those girls so that we can get ahead of the line," Javon suggested.

"Man, you are joking," Scott said.

"Naw, man, we are going to be out here forever with the rest of these noobs. Let's do it."

Marty looked around at the line building up. He blew in the air, watching vapors form in the cold air. "Man, I can see my breath," he said.

"Then why don't you give it a Tic Tac," Javon jokes.

"Ha, ha, ha, good one," Marty said.

Marty turned to Scott. "He's right, Scott, what we got to lose."

Scott thought about it for a minute. He looked back over the girls who were still staring in their direction, talking amongst themselves. "What the hell, roomies, if y'all game I am game," he said.

"My man," Javon said, wrapping his arm around Scott's shoulder pulling him in.

Javon looked at his friend Marty. "Damn, homey. Can you think of warm thoughts? We can't walk over there while you're shaking like a chicken at a meat processing plant."

"Fuck you, homey; it's colder than polar bear shit out here," Marty said. "But I got this," he said, straightening out his posture and puffing out his chest.

Javon laughed. "Warm thoughts' bro," he reiterated.

"Man, I can barely feel my nuts," Marty said.

"Nobody told you to wear those nut huggers," Scott said, referring to Marty's tight slim-leg jeans.

"No, I think they accentuate his tight ass," Javon said in an effeminate voice.

"Fuck you both, let's see who gets more action," Marty said.

"Relax, bro, we just fucking with you," Javon said,

wrapping his arm around Marty and kissing him on his forehead as they made their way over to the group of young women.

"Hey, ladies, what's up? I'm Javon, and these are my homies, Marty and Scott."

"Hi, I am Crystal, and these are my homies Gabby and Pepper," Pepper said, mimicking Javon.

Javon laughed. "Oh, okay, okay, that's what's up," he said.

"We were wondering if we could join you, Queens, and buy y'all a drink when we get inside," Scott said.

"Are you sure y'all are not just trying to cut in line?" Crystal asked.

Scott threw his hands out at them. "Naw, baby, we could never jump in front of royalty like that with that type of disrespect."

Crystal and her girls laughed. Scott was a smooth talker, she thought, and not too bad on the eyes either.

"Listen to him. The white boy got game," Gabby said, looking Scott up and down with a smile on her face.

"Like Mike and Kobe," Scott said as he shot an imaginary basketball in an imaginary hoop.

"I hear you, I hear you," Gabby said, smiling. She was an attractive girl with long wavy black hair and a bright, engaging smile.

"Whatever," Javon said, rolling his eyes at Scott's remark, slightly jealous.

"It's cool, but please don't try to dip on us once we get inside the club," Pepper said.

"No, no, it's not like that, I promise," Javon said, laughing.

"So where y'all from?" Crystal asked as she took a hit off her passion fruit-flavored vape pen and passed it to Gabby.

"Ann Arbor," Javon answered.

"College boys?"

"U of M," Marty responded.

"Where are you guys from?" Scott asked Crystal and her friends.

"Detroit," Crystal lied.

"Oh yeah, what part ?" Javon asked.

"Eastside," Gabby said, continuing the lie that Crystal started.

"Man, y'all don't look like no girls from Detroit's eastside," Javon said skeptically.

"What the hell does an eastside girl from Detroit supposed to look like?" Gabby said, sounding offended.

"He didn't mean anything by it," Scott said, coming to his friend's defense.

Javon interrupted. "No, actually, I did. Like you know the eastside," he said. He leans over and sniffs Crystal, who pulls back.

"What the hell are you doing?" she said, confused.

"You don't even smell like the eastside!" he said, causing Crystal and her friends to burst out laughing.

"Okay, okay, you got us; we are actually from Farmington Hills," Crystal admitted.

"I knew it!" Javon said, laughing as well.

Scott let out a sigh of relief as the tension immediately left the cold night air between them.

"But don't get it twisted. It doesn't make us any less dangerous," Gabby said, shaking her head and finger for emphasis at the same time.

"Hey, we're all friends here," Marty said, laughing nervously.

"ID's out," they all heard a loud booming voice say as they all made their way to the front door. Upon giving entrance into the building, each one of their identification cards was scanned. As they entered the atrium, they were met by another muscular security guard who swept a security wand over them for weapons. Crystal noticed the coat check was to their immediate right and did not look all that secure, so she and her friends removed anything of value from their coat pockets and put it in their purses. Loud Disco music is booming from the first floor level of the club. KC and the Sunshine band's - Do you wanna go party echoed off the walls.

Javon and his two friends watched as Crystal and her girls checked their coats in at the club's coat check.

"Damn! Dawg, look at the jolly rancher on her," Javon said to his boys as Crystal took off her coat, revealing her tight-fitting hot pink mini dress.

"Bootylicious!" Marty said, rubbing his thin mustache.

"Hey, I think she likes you," Marty said.

"You think so?" Javon replied, grinning.

"No, I was referring to Scott," Marty said, laughing as he high-fived Scott.

"Whatever," Javon said. "Chill fool, they're coming back this way."

"I see y'all still here," Crystal said, smiling.

"Yeah, we were about to bounce and get lost in the crowd, but… ouch," Javon said, as Scott elbowed him in the side. "Ignore him. He's just screwing around."

"Drinks on us, ladies."

* * *

The six of them made their way through the crowd on the first floor over to the bar. "You want to do some shots?" Scott asked Crystal and her friends.

"Bring them on, handsome," Crystal said, flirting with Scott as Javon looked on with envy.

"Six shots of Jamerson," Scott ordered after he got the bartender's attention. "I need to see some ID," the bartender asked.

Scott pulled out his driver's license and handed it to the bartender, who looked it over quickly and handed it back to him. "Six shots, coming up," she said.

The bartender sat six-shot glasses on the bar and filled each one with the bottle of Jamerson in her hand. "That will be eighteen dollars," she said. Scott handed her his credit card. "Keep the tab open," he requested as he passed everyone their shot off the bar. "Here's to new friends," he said, raising his shot glass in the air.

"To new friends, the rest of them repeated," as they all

tossed back the shots.

"Aaaahhh! Damn, I can feel the heat coming back to my balls now," Marty said, smiling.

As Scott locked eyes with Gabby, a nervous smile came across his face, damn she was beautiful, he thought. "Do you want to dance?" she asked him, taking him by surprise.

"Sure," he said as he took her hand, and she led him to the dance floor to the sounds of Peaches & Herbs. "Shake Your Groove Thing."

"Bartender another round," Javon said.

"Who's paying?" the bartender asked. "My boy got this," Javon said as he pointed to Scott out on the dance floor and gave him a thumbs up. Scott noticed him, smiled, and gave him the thumbs-up right back.

"See, I told you," Javon said back to the bartender with a mischievous smile on his face. "Attitude," Javon said, smirking as the bartender walked off to get their drinks.

Pepper could feel Marty's eyes on her before he got up the nerve to speak. "Hey, would you like to dance with the Marty man," he asked, smiling and dancing in place. She looked at Marty, who had a wide grin on his dimpled face. He was the shortest out of his two friends and the chubbiest. But Pepper got the impression that did not stop him from thinking he was a lady's man.

"Go Marty, Go," his friend Javon egged him on.

Marty licked his two fingers and rubbed his chest with them while swaying his hips.

Pepper laughed. "I'll dance with you, but please don't

do that move on the floor, pleaseee."

"You got it!" Marty replied, grinning.

Crystal took a hit on her vape pen as she sized Javon up. He was tall with an athletic build and attractive and the most vocal of his small entourage. "So, what's your story?" she asked.

"What do you mean?" he answered as he looked off into the crowd of people and strangers on the dance floor.

"What do you think?" she asked coyly.

"Right now, I am just hanging out with my boys and enjoying the company of some beautiful women, but the night's still young and full of possibilities," he said flirtatiously as the bartender finally poured their second round of shots at the bar.

Crystal smiled. "Okay, okay, I'll drink to that," she said. As she observes their friends coming off the dance floor and headed back over to the bar. They all pick up their shots.

"What are we toasting now?" Scott asked.

"To the creepiest club in Pontiac, maybe in the world!" Crystal said.

"Wait, what in the world are you talking about?" Javon said.

"Come on. You did not hear about this club?" Crystal asked, surprised.

"Hear what?" Scott interceded.

Crystal went silent as the bartender began wiping the bar off in front of them with a towel. "Can I get y'all anything else?" she asked.

"No, we're good for now, thanks," Javon answered back.

He looked back at Crystal. "You were saying?"

"Are you first-timers here?" Crystal asked.

"Yeah, so what," Marty answered.

Crystal and her girlfriends laughed.

"Let me give you guys a little history on this place," Crystal said.

"Please do," Javon said.

"This club use to be a church that was closed down due to numerous allegations of sexual abuse by the clergy as well as satanic rituals and blood sacrifices."

"Get the fuck out of here!" Javon laughed.

"No, seriously, there are people that say that their friends visited this club and were never heard from or seen again," Gabby stated.

"Well, wouldn't the police look into something like this?" Marty asked.

Crystal laughed. "Sure, but no evidence, no case, right."

"Bottoms up!" Gabby said as they all threw back their shots.

Crystal took out her iPhone and typed in mysterious disappearances associated with Nightclub. "Look at this," she said, showing Javon and his friends the news report and other stories related to the same nightclub that they were now occupying.

"This is some crazy shit!" Javon said.

"Yeah, but it also could be a publicity stunt orchestrated by the owner of this club to generate more business," Marty said, skeptical.

"True that," Scott said.

"Man, I gotta pee; anybody else has to go?" Marty asked.

"What? You're scared to go to the restroom alone now, Marty?" Javon teased.

"Of course not," Marty responded sheepishly. "I was just asking, that's all."

Pepper grabbed Marty by the hand. "I'll show you where it's located. Javon, don't be an asshole," she said.

" What? I was just joking," Javon replied.

"Man, Pepper in rare form tonight, she ain't never been this outspoken before," Gabby said, as she took a sip of the beer they just ordered poured in clear plastic cups.

"Don't be an asshole," Javon said, mocking Pepper in a silly effeminate voice.

Scott patted Javon on the back. "Relax, dude, you are an asshole," Scott said, laughing.

Javon looked behind them at the bartender. She was smiling at him weirdly, but what was up with her eyes, he thought? They look all black with no hint of the sclera. "What the fuck?" he mumbled.

"What's wrong?" Scott asked.

Javon pointed at the bartender. " Man, her fucking eyes are zombies out."

"What?"

"Bro, her eyes were all fucking black! Eyeballs and all." He insisted.

"Dude, whatever you are smoking, I want some of that shit," Gabby interjected.

"Here she comes," Javon said with panic in his voice as he noticed the bartender headed over to a small booth with a table that they were now sitting at in the corner.

"You forgot this," she said, handing Scott his credit card.

"Thanks," Scott replied.

"Anything else," she said as she made eye contact with everyone at the booth.

"No thanks, we're good," Scott said.

"You too?" she asked Javon.

Javon swallowed the lump in his throat. "Yea... Yeah... thanks," he stammered. He watched her intensely as she walked away from the table.

Scott took a sip of his beer and shrugged his shoulders. "She looked normal to me," he said.

"Bro, don't you think that was weird that she turned to me and said you too?" Javon asked.

"Yeah, that was weird," Crystal answered before Scott did.

"Maybe she likes you, roomie, I don't know," Scott said.

"Man, where in the hell is Marty and your girl? Did they get lost?" Javon asked.

"You right; they have been gone for a while," Crystal responded, looking at her cell phone.

A commotion suddenly broke out on the dance floor, directing all their attention to what was going on in that area of the club. Unfortunately, all they could see was two large bouncers rush in and pull two guys apart, fighting on the floor over only God knows what. One of the combatants looks worse for the wear than the other with a black eye and a busted lip.

"Wow, First fight for tonight," Gabby said.

After the two patrons were removed from the dance floor and most likely the club itself, the other clubbers filtered back out on the dance floor and began dancing again to the music as if nothing ever occurred.

"Hey, did you see that dude get his ass kick?" Marty asked as he and Pepper returned to the table.

"What did you do fall through the toilet?" Javon asked.

"No, Pepper and I were just getting to know each other better," he said, winking at Pepper, who blushed.

"Whatever," Javon said. "This beer tastes like warm piss."

"Javon saw one of the black-eyed kids," Gabby said.

"No shit! Who?" asked Pepper.

"The bartender," Gabby answered, nodding towards the bar.

"What the fuck is a black-eyed kid?" Javon asked, agitated.

"They are paranormal creatures that disguise themselves as children that appear to people at their homes or parking lots, and their eyes are completely black, including the whites of their eyes," Gabby answers.

Javon took the last sip of his warm piss beer and

crumpled the plastic cup in his hand. "Man, y'all weird as shit!" he said.

"What are you scared of?" Crystal asked.

"I ain't scared of shit!" Javon replied defensively.

"Then I have a proposal," Crystal said, gushing with delight.

"What's that?" Javon asked.

Crystal's face lit up. "Let's hideout in the club after it closes and everybody leaves."

"That's trespassing. Can't we get arrested for that if we get caught?' Marty stated, concerned.

"Not if no one knows we are here," Crystal answered.

"I am in," Gabby said. "Me too," said Pepper.

Scott laughed. "That's crazy, but why not?" he said.

Pepper walked over to Marty and gave him a soft peck on the lips. "Okay, I am in," he said, grinning.

"What the fuck! Seriously?" Javon said, flustered. He grabbed Scott by the arm. "Bro, we need to talk," he said as he escorted Scott away from the booth and the listening distance of Crystal and her friends.

"What's up, Roomie?" Scott asked.

"Are you kidding me, bro? We barely know these Halloween bitches, and you all are talking about hiding out in this nightclub with them after it closes. For all, we know they could be part of a cult and setting us up as sacrificial fucking lambs, for a black mass or some shit!"

Scott busted out laughing. "Come on, are you fucking serious, bro? These girls are just trying to punk us."

"What?" Javon replied.

"Javon, you don't think they are fucking serious, do you?"

Javon looked at Scott, still confused. Was it something that he had missed? Or maybe his friends had been hexed by these broads, he thought.

"Look, bro, we are all getting laid tonight and our pipes wet if we play our cards right, including Marty, who probably hasn't had a piece of ass since he broke up with his girlfriend, Carly."

"That would be about three months ago," Javon said.

Scott placed his hand on Javon's shoulder. "Exactly, if he keeps jerking off, he is going to have arms like Popeye and carpet palms like Bigfoot," Scott said.

Javon laughed. " Ha, ha, ha, that's funny, roomie."

"Bro, just play along, and the next thing you know, you will have Crystal moaning in your ears. Oh,' Javon, Javon," Scott said, leaning into his friend's ear.

Javon grinned. "Yeah, I would like to tap that ass."

Scott laughed. "Get to work, then pimping and stop acting like a Chump."

"Bro, you keep talking like that, and your Wasp ass parents are going to disown your ass," Javon said.

"Yeah, right," Scott replied, smiling.

Crystal walked over to Javon and put her hand on his chest. "So, what's up?" she asked softly.

"I am in," he said. Crystal smiled and took Javon's face into her hands, and began kissing him. He felt himself getting hard as her tongue entered his mouth.

"I knew you'd come around," she said.

"Wow, that was hot!" Pepper said, giggling.

"Our turn," Gabby said to Scott.

Marty jumped up and raised his drink. "Let's get this fucking party started now!" He shouted out excitedly.

Javon looked back over at the bartender. Was it just his imagination, or did she just nod at him with a mischievous smile on her face?

"I knew you would come around," Crystal's voice echoed in his head. But had he made the right decision? His voice asked back in his head.

Javon glanced back over at the bartender serving the other clubbers drinks, and to his relief, she did not lock those blacked out demon eyes on him this time as he studied her from afar.

"You like what you see?" Crystal said, following Javon's glance.

"What?" Javon answered as if he was just awakened out of a hypnotic trance.

Crystal smiled and nodded her head towards the bartender. "No, she's not my type," Javon replied, taking another sip of his drink.

"How do you know?" Crystal asked as she slid her finger across the rim of her glass while seductively gazing into Javon's eyes.

"Because you are," he said, as he returned Crystal's seductive gaze with one of his own whiles at the same time trying to shake the uneasy feeling he had about hiding out inside the nightclub after closing.

"Good answer," she said as she leaned into him and

gave him a peck on the lips.

Scott raised his drink in another toast. "This is for the after party!"

"To the after party!" they all cheered in unison as their glasses clanged together.

Chapter Four

The song "flashlight" by Parliament now reverberated throughout the nightclub bouncing off the walls with the now packed and sweaty crowd of young clubbers on the club's first floor. Ironically, all of them were just spermatozoa in their fathers' balls when the song first came out in the late seventies. The smell of alcohol, cannabis, and sweat permeated the "misty vapor-filled air" produced by the Club's mounted fog machines high above.

Javon and his crew had now made it their business to cover all three floors of the massive nightclub as they went into midnight. If they got tired of the genre of music that one level was playing, they simply and drunkenly made their way to another floor with a different venue. So it was club-hopping to them without the inconvenience of having to leave the club. Crystal and her friends were never too far behind.

* * *

As the night proceeded on into the bewitching hour, the proposal and challenge by their new friends of hiding out in the spacious nightclub with the notorious reputation soon left Javon and his friends' minds, as they simply continue to do what they had come to the club to do and that was have a good time! That is until it was brought up again by Crystal, as they all sat together in a booth on the first floor.

"See that door over there," she said, pointing to an ominous-looking red door across the room through the haze and fog. "Yeah, what about it?" Javon answers back with a tone of disinterest in his voice.

"That door leads to the boiler room!" Crystal replied enthusiastically. "That would be the perfect place to hide out before closing," she suggested.

Javon took a sip of his beer as he looked at Crystal skeptically. "Fuck! There's got to be a million doors in this building; how do you know that one leads to the boiler room?" he asked.

"Move these drinks out of the way," Crystal said, before pulling a small blueprint out of her purse, rolled it out, and laid it out on the table. She shined her iPhone light on the blueprint and pointed to the area that was marked boiler room.

"You gotta be fucking kidding me?" Javon said.

"Her mom's an engineer. So what do you expect?" Gabriella said, grinning.

"You still serious about this, huh?" Marty asked, while hugged up on Pepper in the corner of the booth.

Crystal shook her head yes, snapping her fingers at the same time. "Hell yes, we are! You all ain't chicken shitting out on us, are you?" Her two girlfriends laughed and snapped their fingers in solidarity.

"Hell no, we're down, but you might want to put that

shit away before someone sees it," Scott said, referring to the blueprint.

Crystal laughed and put the blueprint back away in her purse. " Good, I am glad to see I am not the only one with balls at this table!"

"Excuse me?" Javon said, looking at Crystal strangely; his reaction caused Pepper and Gabriella to break out in laughter.

"What's so funny? If I order KFC, I don't want Burger King," he said.

"That's so fuck up!" Gabriella said.

"Damn, can y'all chill out with this politically correct shit crap! You two are killing my buzz," Marty said.

"I can toast to that!" Scott said, raising his beer in the air.

Crystal playfully punched Javon in the side of his arm. "Ouch! He said, grabbing his arm. "Hey, my apologies if I unintentionally offended anyone at this table with or without balls."

"Yes, you can come across as a foot in your mouth, arrogant jock!" Gabriella said.

"Well, it's good to know I made an impression on you, my highness," Javon said with a smirk.

Gabriella smiled back and gave Javon the middle finger.

"Children, Children, let's play nice," Scott joked, trying to de-escalate the building tension in the air at the booth. But at the same time, thinking, "What in the hell was Javon doing? Besides blowing the best night away, they have had out in a long time as roomies together. No! He could not let that happen. Better yet, he would not allow that to happen, he thought.

"Don't worry. You've made quite an impression on me," Crystal whispers in Davon's ear.

"Hey, roomie, let's go grab some drinks for the table," Scott proposed to Javon.

"We can do that," Javon said as he watched Gabriella giving him what he thought was the stink eye. "Fuck you!" he thought.

"I thought we were going to get drinks?" Javon said as he noticed Scott headed in the opposite direction of the bar. "Yeah, we will, but I need to take a piss first," Scott replied.

"A piss or a pee-pee?" Javon jokes, referencing their friend Marty's remark from earlier.

"Both," Scott said.

"Hey, look, man, what are you doing?" Scott said as he put his arm around Javon's shoulder.

"Bro, your girl Gabriella is a real bitch, plus I think she got it in for me," he said.

" Roomie, first, she is not my girl, just some chick that I met tonight, okay?" Scott responded.

Javon nodded his head in agreement.

"Roomie, what is our oath?" Scott said, grinning.

"Bros before Hoes, of course," Javon said softly. "I can't hear you!" Scott said, smiling.

"Bros before Hoes!" Javon shouted out loudly. "That's what I am talking about!" Scott said. "Now, I am not blown away by Crystal's personality either, but they all have one thing in common.

"What's that?" Javon asked.

"Why do you think they want us to spend the night in this club with them?" Scott asked.

Javon's smirk came back on his face. "Because they're fucking creepy, that's why."

Scott smiled. "Maybe, but creepy chicks get horny too," he said. "And I think this is their fantasy to get boned in what they think is a haunted nightclub, and I am proudly up to the task to fulfill that fantasy."

"Bro, that little pecker of yours is going to get you in trouble one day!" Javon said, laughing.

"It already has. Now let's get our heads back into the game MVP," Scott said as he gave Javon a fist bump.

Chapter Five

Javon and Scott inhaled the fragrance of cannabis and cheap perfume and body spray as they made their way down one of the nightclub's dark corridors to a nearby restroom. A line of other young men was already standing outside of the restroom's entrance, waiting to get inside to empty their bladders so that they could make room for the consumption of more alcohol before the night was over. Javon and Scott got in line behind the other men before them.

"Damn, this is one long-ass line," Javon said as he counted at least seven or eight heads in front of them. "Yeah, but it appears to be moving pretty quick," Scott said as he took a joint from behind his ear and lit it up. Javon watches as his friend takes a long toke on the dooby before passing it over to him.

"Hey! Put that out and away," Scott said as he observed a tall and muscular dude with "Security" written across his chest's black t-shirt headed in their direction. "Hey guys, if you are tired of waiting in this line, it's another restroom further down the hall to your right," he said in a deep and authoritative voice.

"Thanks, bro," Javon said as he held the still lit joint behind his back.

The large security guard gave Javon and Scott a quick discretionary glance before proceeding down the dark corridor.

"What in the hell is rent a cop's problem?" Scott said.

"I don't know, and I don't care, but let's see if this other restroom is less busy, I gotta piss like a racehorse," Javon said as he took a drag on the joint and handed it back to Scott.

"I'm with you, roomie; this line smells like *Bold body spray* and ass," Scott said.

The two of them now made their way down the corridor and to the other restroom that was surprising to them unoccupied. Had they been the only ones that had heard the security guard say that "It's another restroom down the hall?" As they made their way inside the surprisingly clean and spacious restroom.

Javon and Scott walked over to two of the six urinals against the wall.

"Damn, bro, that feels good," Javon said as he relieved himself in one of the upright urinals. The urinal motion sensor made a flushing sound when it detected he had finished.

Javon walked over to one of the sinks to wash his hands off. When the restroom lights went out, putting him and Scott into darkness. "What the fuck!" he yelled out. "Goddammit, I think I just pissed on my pants!" Scott said in the dark.

The lights suddenly came back on in the restroom. "Hey, Scott put your little wiener in your pants, and let's get the hell out of here before the lights go back out," Javon said.

The lights flickered in the restroom. "Scott?" Javon said as he turned around to see that his friend was no longer standing at the urinal. The sound of moaning now caught Javon's attention coming from one of the six stalls in the restrooms.

"Yeah fuck me, baby!" he heard what sounded like a female's voice coming from one of the stalls. "Hey, you two need to get a fucking hotel room!" he shouted out as he made out two feet underneath the stall's door. The door to the stall shook violently in synchronicity to the activity behind its door.

"Too deep, Stop! Too deep," he heard the voice now say, over the sound of primal grunts.

Javon's eyes widened as he cautiously approached the door. "She said stop!" he yelled out. Before the stall's door flung open and a large reptilian tail came out like a snake behind it swirling in the air.

The creature's gecko head turned in Javon's direction as its black eyes flickered underneath its bumpy lids; it appeared to smile at Javon with a mouthful of sharp baby daggers, as black drool slithered out of its mouth and dripped down onto the floor.

Javon stumbled back onto the restroom wall in shock! He recognized the man-creature immediately! It was the house deejay, DJ Reptile!

"You next!" the creature said smiling, exposing all its pointy teeth.

"No! No! No! " "Wake up, bro. Wake up!" Scott said as he shook Javon, who was now sitting on the restroom floor.

"What, what, what the hell just happened?" Javon said groggily.

"Man, you must have had a bad trip on that weed or something," Scott said as he helped his friend back onto his feet.

"No, no, did you see it?" Javon asked, pointing in the direction of one of the stall doors that is open.

"Seen what?" Scott answered back, oblivious to what his friend was talking about in his excitement.

"See that giant ass lizard monster, fucking in this restroom, that's what?" Javon responded, visibly upset.

Scott tries to maintain his composure before busting out in laughter.

"Man, you gotta be bullshitting me!" he said.

"No, I am not, and where the fuck was you anyway?" Javon asked, agitated.

"Bro, I was finished, so I step outside. What's the big deal?" Scott answered.

Javon said nothing but left out of the restroom, leaving his friend standing there alone.

"What in the fuck is up with you, roomie? You have been tripping all night," Scott said, throwing his hands up in anguish.

The stall door begins to swing back and forth on its own as if there was an unseen force moving it? Scott walked over to the black stall door and its partitions.

His mouth dropped as he placed his hand on the giant claw marks that were distinct on the door's surface and throughout the inside of the stall. He looked down in the toilet that appeared to be covered in somebody's blood, causing him to recoil back in fear. "Javon!" Scott screamed out as he ran out of the restroom.

"Bro, we need to get the fuck out of here now!" Scott said as he met up with Javon, who was still waiting for him on the outside.

"What did you see?" Javon asks. Scott did not respond. He only looked at his friend with a blank look on his face. "What did you see?" Javon shouted out! "I don't know," Scott said, confused, looking back towards the restroom with fear in his eyes.

"Show me," Javon said as he slowly made his way back into the restroom with Scott behind him.

The restroom appeared as it did when they first entered. Scott walked over to the stall door that was now closed. He opened it and looked inside, and on its surface for the claw marks, they were gone. Scott looked down at the surface of the toilet; there was no blood on the lid and below. He looked back up at Javon with a look of befuddlement on his face. "What?" Javon asked. "They are gone?" he answers. "What is gone?" Javon replied.

"The claw marks and the blood," said Scott, baffled. "The claw marks and the blood," he repeated softly.

Chapter Six

Javon and Scott made their way back to their party's table without speaking another single word about the strange events that had transpired in the club's restroom. One thing for sure, though, Javon had decided that there was no way in hell that he now was going to go alone with Crystal's and her girlfriends' insane plans to hide out and spend the night in this joint. No way in hell! As far as he was concerned, no piece of punani on this planet was worth the risk of spending the night in this strange place. He glances over at the bar across from them only to see that the bartender with the peculiar eyes was now gone and replaced by another bartender in her place.

"Damn baby, I missed you; what took you so long?" Crystal asked as Javon sat back down in the booth beside her reluctantly. "Trust me; you don't want to know," he said as his eyes went over to DJ reptile on the stage in his booth doing his thing, he could feel his heart fluttering in his chest at the mere sight of him.

Scott's eyes followed him nervously.

"Did that fuck ever leave that deejay booth?" Javon asks, pointing discreetly at DJ reptile.

"What? No. He has been up there putting out this badass music since you two went to the little boys' room,"

Gabriella answers, taking a sip of her drink.

"That's not possible," Javon replied.

"Are we missing something here?" Pepper interjected.

"Yeah, Javon swore he has just seen that deejay banging the shit out of some babe in the restroom we just left," Scott chimed in.

"No shit!" Crystal said, smiling. "DJ reptile was getting his freak on, huh?" Marty said, laughing.

"Not funny, asshole, it looked like he was abusing her," Javon said.

"Bro, chill. I was just kidding," Marty said.

"Are you talking about rape?" Gabriella asks, concerned.

Javon put his hands on his head as if he had a headache. "I don't know what I saw in the bathroom? He did not even look human," he said.

"What? You're not making any sense Javon," Pepper injected.

"Yes, he is. I told you this place was haunted!" Crystal said with glee in her voice.

"There is something else," Scott said with a tone of slight hesitation in his voice.

"What?" Crystal asks.

Scott picked up the drink in front of him and downed the last remnants in one gulp before he continued on with his declaration.

"I saw these strange claw marks in the stall and blood where Javon told me he had seen DJ lizard or whatever his name is assaulting this girl, and then when we looked again, and I saw nothing!"

" Well, all I know is DJ reptile has not moved his ass from that spot since you both took your Hardy Boys and Nancy Drew mysteries asses to the bathroom," Pepper said sarcastically.

"Who in the hell is the Hardy Boys?" Marty asks, grinning.

" I think what you two seen was apparitions," Crystal said.

"Appar… what?" Javon said, scratching the side of his head.

"Ghost, spirits, specters - jughead!" Gabriella said. "Manifestations of the netherworld that are not at rest," she continued in an intentionally creepy voice with her impression also of weird music to accompany her definition.

"You are fucking bugging. I am outta here!" Javon said as he stood up to leave.

"You two coming?" he said, looking at Scott and Marty. Who he could not believe was still sitting at the table with these wannabe ghost hunters whom he was sure did not have a fucking clue what they were getting their pretty little heads into, no ideal.

"Homey come on," Scott said. Javon's eyes narrowed; it was now or never as far as he was concerned for both of his roomies to show where their true loyalty lay and to whom. "Bros over Hoes."

"Marty?" Javon said.

"Ah fuck it! We gotta go," Scott said to Gabriella.

"Marty, get your fat ass up!" Javon barked. Marty looked nervous and stood up. But despite his nervousness, he still felt he had to save face in front of Pepper, and although he knew physically he was no match for Javon, he would not allow Javon to make him look like a punk in front of everybody at the table.

"You are not my fucking father. Don't talk to me like that!" he said, standing up for himself.

Javon smiled. "Well, what are you going to do about it? Body by Blubber," he said, taunting Marty.

"Fuck you, asshole!" Marty shouted back at him.

Scott quickly threw his arms out to separate the two of them. Before, the situation escalated any further. "What in the weird cosmic fuck is going on here? You two are good friends, do you hear your damn selves," he said.

"He's body-shamed me!" Marty shouted back. With a pouting and embarrassed look on his face. That made it even worse when he could have sworn he heard one of the girls giggling.

"I don't give a flying squirrel's left nut. You both need to chill! We are brothers, remember?" Scott said as he gave both of his friend's fist bumps in camaraderie.

"My apologies, bro, I didn't mean to body shame you," Javon said, extending his fist as an act of forgiveness. "You're still an asshole," Marty said as he gave Javon a conciliatory fist bump.

"I know," Javon said with a grin on his face. "Now, let's go," he said.

"Twelve thousand dollars!" Crystal shouted out.

"What?" Scott said, looking over at Crystal, confused.

"We all can make twelve-thousand dollars if we can spend one night in this place and have legitimate proof that we did!" she said.

"What in the hell are you talking about?" Javon asks.

"I was keeping this quiet until we all follow through, but I have a proposal from a legitimate source that if a group of my friends and I spent overnight in this place and showed legitimate proof that we had done so, the prize for our effort would be twelve thousand dollars!"

"She's bullshitting!" Javon said skeptically.

"Am I?" Crystal said as she reached in her purse, pulled out a stack of twenty-dollar bills wrapped in a money band, and handed it to Javon, who took it from her with his mouth wide open.

Javon sat back down at the table with the cash in his hand, nervously looking around to make sure no one was watching them. He looked at the money band that said three thousand dollars.

"Girl, why in the hell are you walking around with this kind of money in your purse?" Javon asks as Scott took the stack of twenties out of his hand to examine them and then passed it on to Marty.

"Let's just say it's a cash advance payment from our sponsor," Crystal replied, smiling, as she stroked Javon's face softly.

"So you were holding out on us?" Marty said.

Maybe their friend Marty wasn't as dumb as he looked, Crystal thought as she took the wad of cash from him and placed it back inside her oversized purse. But his remark did little to take her off her stride. "No, we wanted to know if we could trust you," Crystal said, with a nod of approval from her girlfriends.

"Are you still leaving lover?" Crystal asks Javon. Javon looked over at his boys Scott and Marty. He had had a bad feeling about this place all night long. But damn it, it was 1:30 in the morning, and if he hid out in the club for four more hours with these batty bitches he would be two-thousand dollars more prosperous, he thought - easy money.

Javon took a deep breath and exhaled. "Fuck it! I am in," he said for the second time that night.

Crystal smiled. " Good, you won't regret it," she said.

"Even split?" Scott asks. "Even Split," Crystal answered. "Now, if you all don't have any more questions, I think we need to get our sweet asses down to that boiler room and start earning this money," she proposed.

Chapter Seven

As soon as one of the security guards covering the area over by the boiler room door left the area to respond to another fight that had broken out in a different location inside the club. With their newfound friends in tow, Crystal and her crew seized upon the moment and made their way expeditiously over to the door.

"Damn, it's locked," Scott said as he attempted to open the door. "No problem," Gabriella said as she removed a lock pick set from her purse and quickly went to work on the door knob lock. "Click!" Gabriella smiled and turned the door knob, opening the heavy door slightly. "Damn girl, you good!" Crystal said, grinning.

"Do you always carry one of those on you?" Javon asks, looking down at the lock pick in Gabriella's hand. "Don't everyone?" Gabriella answers with a smirk on her face as she puts the lock pick set back into her hand purse.

"Let's go," Crystal said. Pepper was the last to go through the door that they had opened just wide enough to slide each of their bodies through the gap. Pepper looked around one last time before the lights went dim in the club as she shut the red door behind them.

* * *

The basement to the boiler room was dimly lit as they now all made their way cautiously down the old concrete stairs into the bowels of the building. "Do you know where you are going?" Javon asks Crystal.

Crystal put her finger to her mouth. "Hey, keep it down, will you? We might not be the only ones down here," she whispered. "And yes, I have a pretty good idea where we are in the building."

Crystal shone a pocket flashlight on one of the pressure gauges on one of the water pipes causing it to illuminate in the dimly lit basement. The boiler room not only had a dank and musty smell to it that hung in the rank air but ominous energy that's not lost on its present visitors.

As the group of trespassers made their way into another enclave of the previous church's colossal basement, an icy cold breeze suddenly swept through, sending a weird chill through most of them.

"Damn, did you feel that?" Pepper asks nervously as she folded her arms together for warmth. "Yeah, I wonder where that cold gust of wind came from," Gabriella answered.

Scott laughed and just shrugged off their concerns. "You gotta be kidding me. It's a basement. It is supposed to be drafty. That breeze could have come from anywhere down here."

"Look, we need to split up in pairs and hide out. It is not wise for all of us to be together if we get discovered," Crystal said. Javon shook his head in disapproval. "You gotta be kidding me? I guess you have never seen a horror movie in your life," he said.

"No, I have seen plenty," Crystal shot back. "Well, then you should know that is the second dumbest fucking ideal that you've had all night!" Javon replied to the grinning faces of his friends.

"And what was the first one?" Crystal asks, not one to back down from anyone, especially someone she barely knew.

Javon looked around at the basement and back at the faces of everyone standing there in the boiler room. "I am still debating that one, but so far, it's not looking good if you must know," he said.

His boy Scott leaned into him and whispered in his ear. "Bro, if you keep this up, you are not getting laid tonight."

"Scott, seriously? We are in a church, bro!" Javon replied.

"Was a church," Scott corrected.

"Whatever, we still need to split up in pairs, so who are you going with?" Crystal asks Javon, catching him off guard.

"What?" Javon replied.

"I said who are you going with?" Crystal asks again, arms folded and with what Javon detected as an "I don't give a fuck attitude on her face."

"I guess I am stuck with you," he answers. Crystal stuck her lip out, making a pouty face. "It's not that bad, is it?" she said, mocking Javon.

He wanted to tell her to go fuck herself but thought better of it under the circumstances since he had voluntarily decided to play her game, at least until daybreak.

"Okay bitches be careful, and we will meet back up here at 3:00 am." Crystal stated.

"Did she just call me a bitch?" Scott whispers to Javon.

"Bro, I don't think she is wrapped too tight. But be careful," Javon advised his friend.

Scott smirked. "Me? Hell, you are the one that's paired up with Ms. Loony Tunes," he said softly.

"Let's go have some fun, baby," Gabriella said, tugging on Scott.

"Yeah, you two deserve each other all right," Javon said as he watched Scott compliantly walk off with Miss's big mouth. Marty looked over at Pepper with a wide grin on his face. "This is a big place, ready to do some exploring." "Ready when you are," she said, taking his hand.

Chapter Eight

The creaking sound of the pipes and other weird noises echoed throughout the boiler room as Marty and Pepper made their way through the different corridors of the basement, which now appeared to be more like a dungeon that went on forever. Finally, the two of them arrived at a door painted with a thick coat of black latex paint that almost looks like it was coated with tar. A yellowish light illuminated from underneath the door. Catching both of their attention. "Jeez, you think someone else is down here?" Marty asks softly.

"I don't know," Pepper answered in the same soft tone of voice. As another cold gust of wind sent a chill down both of their backsides, causing them to shiver at the same time. "You felt that too," Pepper asks, rubbing the side of her arms for warmth. Then it hit her. "Shit, I forgot my coat!" she said.

"Wait, I thought Crystal checked all of your coats out earlier," Marty said.

"She did, but… Pepper stopped talking as her eyes went over to a corner of the room where she spotted her jacket folded up on the floor. She walked over and picked it up. "How in the hell did my jacket get down here?" she asks with a look of confusion on her face.

"Maybe your friend Crystal put it down here when you weren't looking," Marty suggested.

"Maybe," Crystal agreed as she looked back at the door with the same nervousness in her eyes that she had in her voice.

"Let me," Marty said as he put Pepper's coat over her back and shoulders.

"Thank you," she said. It was good to know that Marty could be a gentleman, although she knew his main objective was to get into her pants like a hoe.

"Shall we," he said, looking at the foreboding door in front of them.

Pepper gently rubbed Marty's chin teasingly. " Why not? It might be a good place for us to get comfortable, if you know what I mean," she teased.

A wide smile came across Marty's round face. "I know exactly what you mean," he said. Marty's attention went back to the door; a lump formed in his throat as he slowly reached out for the door knob while at the same time trying to hide his fear from Pepper and appear more formidable than he actually was in her eyes. As the tips of his fingers touched the door knob, the door suddenly flung open, causing both of them to jump back in fright away from the door.

"Shit! What the hell was that?" Marty asks. His heart was now racing in his chest. "Probably just the wind," Pepper said with a nervous giggle, trying to conceal her fear and building anxiety.

"Maybe we should get the hell out of here and leave,"

Marty proposed. "Are you chickening out on me?" Pepper said.

"No, I just don't want anything to happen to you," he said defensively.

"Marty, don't worry about me. I can take care of myself!" Pepper said confidently.

"I didn't mean it that way," he replied. Pepper's back was now facing the open doorway. "Are we going to Chitter-Chatter all night, or do you wanna fuck?" she asks, completely catching Marty by surprise with her remark. "What did you just say?" Marty ask. "You heard me, Spud," Pepper replied, smiling.

"What did you just call me?" Marty asks.

"Spud," Pepper said, grinning. Her eyes now looked strange to Marty, like they had changed and gotten darker, mean, evil.

"How did you know the childhood nickname that the other kids use to tease me and address me by," he asks, confused.

A sinister and twisted smile now formed on Pepper's face. "Because everyone knows who you are, Spud! A fat baked potato that is trying to get some pussy!" she said in a deep masculine voice before she burst out in maniacal laughter.

"Fuck you!" Marty said, tears welling up in his eyes; he was a fool, he thought. Because he had believed this girl actually liked him.

"Marty, why are you talking to me like that?" Pepper said in a different voice, her own.

"Pepper? What? You just freaking insulted me!" he retorted.

"Marty, what in the hell are you talking about?" Pepper asks, appearing oblivious to what had just transpired between them.

"You just... he said, as laughter suddenly erupted from the darkness of the doorway. But he noticed strangely and right away it was the same voice that had come from Pepper. As Pepper slowly turned around to face the door, a long pair of wretched clawed hands attached to unnaturally long and decaying arms shot out and pulled her inside the doorway as she screamed out in anguish! "No!" Marty shouted out to no avail as he ran towards the doorway in an attempt to rescue his friend. Only to find himself falling off the edge beyond it into a dark abyss as his screams punctuated the pitch blackness before he hit the soft Terra below with a resounding thud.

Chapter Nine

Scott and Gabriella had found a small office surprisingly tucked away in the boiler room that they were now hiding out inside. It even had a mini-fridge inside with cold beer that they took the opportunity to remove and drank with no intentions of compensating the fridge's owner, although they would be thousands of dollars richer in the morning.

"Did you just hear that?" Gabriella asks as she sits on top of the office desk.

"Hear what?" Scott said, sitting in front of her in the office's chair smoking a joint.

"It sounded like I heard a scream!" Gabriella said as she got up off the desk quickly and headed towards the door.

"Gabby, hold up! It's probably just the guys screwing with us," Scott said, unconcerned.

" You think? What if someone is in trouble?" she said, still worried.

"Naw, I don't think so; we just need to stay in here and chill out until it's time to meet our friends back up at 3:00 am," he said reassuringly.

Bam! Bam! Bam! A loud pounding on the door suddenly erupted, startling Gabriella causing her to jump back from the door as she shot Scott over a nervous glance. Scott returns the same back to her that quickly broke into a smile on his face to her surprise!

"Man, they almost got me!" he said, laughing.

"What are you talking about?" Gabriella asks, confused by his reaction.

Scott frowned his face up. "Seriously? Can you not see someone is trying to screw with us," he said.

Bam! Bam! Bam! The pounding on the door grew louder, this time startling Scott, which caused Gabriella to laugh to his embarrassment.

"Fuck this shit!" he growled. "Who is it?" he shouted out. Bam! Bam! Bam! They both watched as, this time, the violent pounding on the door caused dents to appear in the metal door. Gabriella screamed out in fear and picked up a Louisville slugger for protection that she had spotted earlier inside the maintenance office, leaning upright against the wall. Scott grabbed a gargoyle-inspired paperweight off the office desk to use as a weapon as he cautiously approached the door.

"Hey, guys, stop fucking around! You're scaring Gabby," he shouted out.

"Really?" Gabriella said to Scott before she gave him a "you gotta be kidding me look." Gabriella nodded her head towards the door. "Go ahead, tough guy, don't stop now," she said condescendingly. But as Scott reached for the door knob to open it, the door quickly flung open on its own, causing him to recoil back in panic as a cold gust of wind followed and entered the office, dropping the temperature in the air.

"Okay, good one," Scott said as he nervously peeped outside the door down the boiler room corridor while still holding the paper weight over his head, ready to launch it at anything or anyone that comes his way.

"Damn, it's cold in here," Gabriella said, rubbing her arms as she now felt the biting chill that hung in the air. The gargoyle paper weight in Scott's hand now took on an eerie yellowish pulsating glow. Scott immediately felt the uncomfortable radiating heat from the paper weight and threw it to the floor, smashing it in pieces!

"Fuck! That thing just burned my hand!" Scott yelled out to Gabriella, who was looking down in horror at the floor while he was nursing the red blisters forming on his hand's palm. Scott's eyes followed Gabriella's to the floor in front of them to the large black monstrous clawed footprints formed in front of them by an entity that they could not see physically creating them. One footprint impression in front of the other leading up the wall of the room. They both watched, mystified as the last footprint formed.

"Scott, we need to go now!" Gabriella said as she looked on in shock.

Scott turned to Gabriella and to her surprise, started laughing.

"What's so damn funny?" she asks.

"Damn bro, y'all almost had me!" he said to no one in particular.

"Scott, what are you talking about?"

"Have you lost your mind? We need to go," Gabriella reiterated.

"Gabby, these are nothing more than parlor tricks," he said confidently.

"What?" she asks.

"Parlor tricks, Special effects, this ain't nothing more than a goddamn haunted house rigged up, fronting as a nightclub," he said, grinning as he made his way over to the wall to examine in his mind the fake monstrous footprints.

"I don't know how they did the hot paper weight thing? But the footprints are probably just a Halloween projection trick," he said.

"Boy, you're tripping, we need to go!" Gabriella insisted. The sound of something growling suddenly erupted in the room.

"Damn, they got sound effects too," Scott said laughing, as he moved his ear closer to the wall to detect where the growling was coming from? Closer to the wall... when the door suddenly slammed shut in the room, followed by the smell of something burning that now hung oppressively in the air. Scott and Gabriella's attention went towards the door. Gabriella rushed over to open the door, but it would not bulge.

"Shit! I think we are locked inside," she said with a look of alarm on her face. Scott tugged at the door as well, but it would not give.

"You smell that?" Gabriella said, referring to the burnt smell. "Yeah, it smells like sulfur," Scott answered.

His mind now started to doubt that this was a prank after all that was being played on them.

"One, two, buckle my shoe, three, four, don't open that door, said a voice in the room."

"What in the hell?" Scott said softly as he and Gabriella turned around to face what appeared to be a young altar boy standing in the corner of the room with his back towards them.

"How did you get in here?" Gabriella asks him. "One, two, buckle my shoe, three, four, don't open that door," he repeated, ignoring her inquiry.

Gabriella slowly approached the boy and placed her hand on his shoulder. "What do you mean?" she asks. The altar boy slapped her hand off his shoulder and spun around quickly, revealing a face of rot and decay with eyeless sockets. "You are all going to hell!" he roared out in a deep guttural voice before dissipating into thin air to the screams of Gabriella and Scott.

The growling started again, but this time it was closer. Scott's and Gabriella's eyes went slowly to the glowing red eyes of two large black rottweilers foaming from the mouth, staring them down menacingly across the room, ready to rip their throats out. They both watched as the dogs drool hit the floor, as the drool did not dissipate.

Chapter Ten

Marty did not know how long he had been unconscious as he slowly came to as he struggled to get back onto his feet in the darkness. All he knew is that he had fallen from something? And his left ankle hurt like a sonofabitch! Panic suddenly kicked in when he realized Pepper was no longer with him! That something or someone? Had snatched her through the door and taken her off to only God knows where? How could he have let that happen? He thought as guilt set in.

"Pepper! Pepper!" he cried out between grunts of pain as he hobbled through the darkness trying to make out where exactly he was in the nightclub. He patted his jacket's pocket for the Mini Maglite that Crystal had supplied each one of them with after confiscating their cellphones. A sigh of relief instantly came over him when he found it and discovered that he did not lose it in the fall.

Click! Click! "Shit!" he mumbled to himself as the flashlight did not come on. He slapped it against his palm aggressively before pushing the on button again. Click! A beam of light finally shot out from it, illuminating a gravestone.

Marty's mouth dropped open as he realized now where he was at and what he had fallen into a cemetery!

A cemetery with endless headstones that seemed to go on forever! "No way," he said to himself as he pinched himself to make sure that he was not dreaming and trapped in a nightmare! He did it harder a second time with his eyes closed. But to his disappointment, only to be faced with the same results as he reopens his eyes. Because cognitively, his brain could not comprehend or understand how he could be in a nightclub one minute and the next a desolate cemetery. "Pepper!" he shouted out again as he listened to his voice echoing in the darkness. Marty could now feel his blood pressure rising, hear his own heart pounding as an ominous fear began to set in that he may not make it out of this place alive. Damn! His ankle hurt like shit! He thought as beads of sweat began to form on his forehead. Suddenly an ear-piercing bird-like shriek broke through the night air, rattling him even more as he stumbled and then regained his footing. "Aaaaharkkk!" "What the fuck was that?" Marty blurted out! Frighten as he waved his flashlight erratically in the night air in search of where the mysterious shrieking noise had come from in the darkness? A noise that did not sound like any animal or creature that he had heard before.

"Aaaaharkkk!" Marty looked above his head, terrified! As he attempted to pick up his pace. He heard what now sounded like the flapping of wings nearby. Marty screamed out in pain! As something sharp scraped the back of the neck, instantly drawing blood as it whooshed by stealthily over his head. "What in the fuck was that?" Marty yelled out in anguish as he reached back and felt the blood now running down his neck.

Marty looked on in horror as the gravestones surrounding him begin to tremble and crack as the ground above them begin to collapse and sink back into the earth. He watched, speechless as a decayed hand shot up out the dirt, proceeded by the arm attached to it! Then the head and body as his flashlight illuminated the corpse exposing rotting and decayed flesh with a skull-like head attached to it dangling on a bony neck that vaguely resembled anything that was once human or alive for that matter.

"Javon! Scott!" he now cried out to his friends in anguish and for help.

"Marty, is that you? Please help me! Help me!" a voice answered back in the darkness.

"Pepper?" he responded as he waved the flashlight around to see what direction her voice had come from in the darkness.

Marty looked up at the gray night sky above him that appeared to be moving, no swirling, wait impossible, he thought. But it was not the sky that was moving but hundreds, maybe thousands of giant bat-like creatures swirling around him in the air like vultures that were making that shrilling sound – Aaaaharkkk! He felt the red pinpoints of their eyes homing in down on him right before something grabbed him fiercely by the collar, taking him violently down to the ground before it began ripping and tearing into the back of his neck with its teeth.

Chapter Eleven

Javon's hands cupped Crystal's breasts as she rode every inch of him inside of her with what he thought was the skill of a seasoned skank. Her tight little banging body met him stroke for stroke as he tried to hold back as long as he could before Javon found himself climaxing inside of that hot box that she was throwing on him with the fierceness of any college wild cat that he had encountered and bedded. "Damn, that was good," he said with a shit-eating grin on his face.

Crystal looked at him, puzzled. "Damn! You came already?" she asks dejectedly.

"Yeah, didn't you?" he answers confidently.

"No!" Crystal said with a frown on her face. "That's okay. I know what you can do for me, minute man," she said smiling.

"Oh, no! You got me twisted. I don't go downtown on the first date," Javon said defensively.

Crystal's eyes lit up. "No, I wasn't asking for that. But you do look like a brownie eater.

"A what?" Javon said, removing his hands off of Crystal's breast.

"You know, a brownie eater," Crystal said, still smiling.

"No, I don't know, and you gotta be out of your mind if you think I am eating your funky…

Crystal broke out laughing. "Relax, I am just fucking with you!" she said as she began to put her clothes back on.

"Whoa, I thought you were serious for a minute," Javon said, laughing.

"But if you really wanted to, I would not stop you," Crystal said with a sly smile on her face.

"No, I don't want to, and please don't ask again," Javon said, offended as he zipped his pants up.

"Boy, for someone that did not make me come, you sure are touchy, touchy," Crystal said as she applied her lipstick.

"Well, that's a low blow," Javon said.

"Yeah, it is, but you tried, right?" Crystal said, blowing Javon a kiss playfully that he did not reciprocate.

Man, who did this crazy bitch think she was? Javon thought as he stared angrily at Crystal for her remark. Did she think she ruled the world because her family had money? That she could talk down to people anyway, she wanted to? All he wanted to do now was hook back up with his roomies, get the money she promised, and put this night and her behind him.

"Whatever," he answers weakly. Crystal smiled.

"Can I join you two?"

Javon's eyes widened as he turned to face the person that had entered the room undetected.

The bartender? Why had he not noticed before how gorgeous she was? He thought.

"My, oh my, how did you get down here?" Crystal asks her, still smiling.

The bartender walked over to Crystal while still keeping her seductive gaze on Javon and planted a soft kiss on Crystal's lips. "The same way you two did. But I won't tell if you don't tell," she answers in a sensual voice.

"Scout's honor," Crystal said, mesmerized by her as well as her perfect red ruby lips that tasted like sweet strawberries to Crystal when she kissed her softly. "Yes, Scout's honor," the bartender said with a mischievous smile on her face.

The bartender then begins unbuttoning her top as Javon and Crystal looked on in amazement and lust. "I want you both," she said to the two of them.

Crystal followed suit and began removing her top as well. She turned toward Javon and smiled. The bartender's top fell to the floor as she motioned to Javon to remove his clothes. She now appeared to have them both under her spell as she took Crystal in her mouth again while they both cupped each other's breasts. "Damn," Javon mumbled to himself as he looked on at the hottest girl-on-girl action he had seen in a long time, and yes, soon Mr. Lucky would be making love to both of them and having the time of his life… so he thought.

Javon strolled over to them as he felt the heat of the bartender's eyes survey his ripped body. "Not bad, star boy," she said with a smile as she welcomed him into the action between her and Crystal. The bartender took

Javon's face into her hands, staring into his eyes as her hot tongue shot into his mouth like a serpent's sending shock waves throughout his body as he hardened under her embrace. He was sandwiched between the two women as the bartender stroked his chest as she went slowly down to her knees, taking him inside that perfect mouth of hers as she felt his body shivering under her control.

Javon could feel Crystal behind him with her lips on his neck and her hands on his ass. He cried out in pain as he felt Crystal's teeth suddenly sink into his neck, causing him to react defensively with a back elbow to her face, which sent her toppling to the ground.

"What the fuck is wrong with you?" he cried out as he felt the blood profusely running down his neck. His eyes widened as he noticed a piece of his flesh, a piece of his neck between Crystal's clenched bloody teeth.

Crystal laughs and spits his flesh out towards him, revealing a mouth full of jagged teeth. Javon looked on in shock as she broke into a wide grin, as her face began to contort into a grotesque and monstrous mask. Javon screamed out in pain again as something sharp ripped into his backside! Its claws shredded the flesh off his back down to his buttocks.

"What in the fuck!" he yelled out as he swung at the bartender, who quickly evaded his blow and jumped behind Crystal, grabbing her in a choke hold. How could someone move that fast, Javon thought. Hell, he was a star athlete, and he doubted he could move that quickly, that animal-like.

Crystal's face suddenly changed back to normal as

she struggled to breathe. "No, please don't harm her!" Javon shouted out in Crystal's defense.

"But the bitch bit you!" the bartender replied in a sinister tone of voice.

Crystal's face was beginning to turn blue from the choke hold as she struggled to break the bartender's vice-like grip on her neck.

"I don't care," Javon shot back as he attempted to put his clothes back on while at the same time negotiating the release of his friend.

"You don't care?" the bartender asks, smiling as her pupils dilated and went utterly black like the hair on a crow's body. "I don't either," she said before she gave Crystal's head one quick jerk, breaking her neck.

"Nooooooo!" Javon screamed out, horrified as he watched Crystal's body fall lifelessly to the ground after being released.

He looked up at the bartender, who was still smiling, her soulless eyes to him did not appear to belong to a human being but something demonic or alien.

"I am going to fucking kill you!" he said, rushing towards her to attack before another sharp pain shot up his belly, now causing severe cramps that sent him toppling over in pain! "What in the fuck did you do to me?" he asks in excruciating pain as he watched his hands begin to blister and swell up. His entire body felt like it was on fire, and his organs were boiling from the inside out.

"What… what… is happening to me?" he cried out in despair as one of his eyeballs popped out of his head and slid down his face in a gooey mush.

"What's the problem, Javon? I thought you like good head," the bartender said as she opened her mouth, revealing a nest full of maggots crawling around inside.

"I put my little buddies inside of you, star boy, and now they are trying to get out!"

"Let them out!" she said.

"No, No, No!" Javon shouted out as he tugged inside of his earlobe, pulling out a giant maggot that was trying to get out. He watched with one eye as the wormy creature that appeared to have the face of the bartender smile at him. He smashed it with his hand into a bloody and yellowish pulp. Javon looked over at Crystal, who was now sitting in the lotus position with her head awkwardly bent to the side, her eyes her face void of any color, a ghastly pallor.

"Crystal?" he mumbled.

"They are coming for us, Javon," she said, grinning through rotten and distorted teeth.

"Crystal, get help! I am hurt!" Javon cried out as he crawled on the floor, coughing up gobs of those slithering little beasts inside of him.

Crystal's head flopped to the other side of her shoulder as if it was not attached to her broken neck. Her cloudy eyes, milk-white, went towards the door as loud footsteps could now be heard coming from the outside. "It won't be long now," she said to Javon, who was dying in agony and pain. "It won't be long now," she repeated, grinning.

Epilogue

The song "Disco Duck" now blared through the nightclub Tentacles, slowly awaking all six of the stowaways that were now altogether in a room in the nightclub called the red room.

"Is it 3:00 am yet?" Marty asks, yawning as he slowly comes to consciousness like the rest of his friends around him.

"I thought I was dead?" Javon said as he patted his chest and stomach to see if he was still alive! His hand then went quickly up to his face. Javon broke out in a wide grin as he realized that he had not suffered any injury to his face, and both his eyeballs were still intact and inside his head.

"No way, I knew it was a dream, I knew it," he repeated.

"Dead? What are you talking about, roomie?" Scott asked Javon, who did not answer but appeared lost in his thoughts.

Gabriella stood up and looked around the dimly lit room that gave off an ominous reddish glow. Visually everything in the room looked red, including the furniture and altar in front of them.

I thought I had died too," Marty said cryptically.

"Me too," Pepper said, shaken.

Crystal walked over to the only door visible in the room, an enormous vault-like door, and pulled its handle. The door would not budge. She looks nervously back at her friends. "Shit! I think we are locked in!"

"No way," Javon said as he rushed over to the door and gave it one good kick that barely rattled the door. Next, he grabbed the wrought iron door handle and began tugging at it, but the only thing he could accomplish was the blisters on his fingers from pulling on the handle.

"Fuck! It's like trying to move a bull!" he said about the door.

"You're not telling me we are locked in this place, are you?" Marty asks fearfully.

"What in the hell is wrong with you people?" Pepper shouted out, drawing everyone's attention in the red room, and bringing them to a standstill. "How in the hell did we all end up in this room? And where are we?" she asks.

"Good question, I have seen situations like this in fucking scary movies, and it's never a good outcome. The worst part is the black friend is always the first one to expire," Javon said, looking around the room nervously.

"Yeah, that's like white privilege at its worst," Gabrielle said, rolling her eyes.

"Exactly if we are going to die, I think the odds of us getting killed should be fucking equal," Javon said.

"Bro, you are talking crazy, ain't none of us going to

die," Scott replied.

"Easy for you to say, but news flash Scott. Talking Ebonics do not make you black," Javon said.

"Look, roomie, I appreciate the cultural lessons, I really do, but don't you think we should be trying to find a way the hell out of here?" Marty said.

"Do you hear that?" Gabrielle asks.

"Where in the hell is Crystal? Javon asks the others as he suddenly notices that she was no longer in the room with them.

"I don't know? But she was standing right beside us," Pepper said with a look of fright on her face.

"Crystallll!" they all began to cry out their friend's name. "Crystal!"

"Shhhhh! Do you hear that?" Gabrielle asks again.

"It sounds like singing... no chanting," Javon stated as the sound of a spotlight coming on echoed through-out the large room. It immediately illuminated the altar, whereas they could now see hundreds of red and white candles burning around the altar.

They all watched, terrified as two ominous cloaked figures approached the altar from out of the darkness, their faces entirely concealed by their cloak's huge hoods.

"Who in the hell are you?" Javon shouted out to the two cloaked figures behind the altar that did not respond when questioned. Then, another cloaked figure appeared out of what seemed like nowhere and walked towards the altar carrying a large gold goblet raised in the air. Javon and the rest of his friends continue to watch in silence and awe as that figure sets the goblet on top of the altar in front of the other two.

The sound of another spotlight coming on reverberated throughout the room. As the red room's five captives now looked on in shock and horror at dozens of other cloaked figures surrounding them like a sentry on each side of them chanting ceremoniously in Latin. The cloaked goblet carrier turned around, facing them at the bottom of the altar.

One of the two cloaked sentry's reigning above her picked up the gold goblet and drank out of it, and passed it to the other one who did the same.

"Hail Satan!" all the cloaked members in the room said in unison.

Javon turned to his friend Scott who looked as if all the blood had drained from his face. In an almost catatonic state like the rest of his fellow stowaways.

"Now, do you believe this was a bad fucking idea!" Javon said to his friend.

"Silence!" one of the cloaked figures at the head of the altar shouted out in a large, booming, and commanding voice. The two authorities at the altar removed their hoods from their heads, revealing their faces and identities, distinguishing looking and middle-aged professionals.

Some of the sect members begin laughing and throwing packs of money at Javon, Scott, and the others.

The female head at the altar smiled. "Payment as promised," she said.

"You can't get away with this shit! People will come

looking for us!" Pepper shouted out as she picked up one of the packs of money and hurled it back at one of the robed members.

"I wanna go home!" she cried out in anguish as tears began rolling down her face.

The two altar heads looked down pleasingly at the goblet carrier, who this time spoke. " Wow, Mom, Dad, that's what the last ones said."

The goblet carrier then removed her cloaked hood, revealing her face as she looked directly over at their guests, their sacrifices.

Pepper looked at the goblet carrier, in shock as she called out her name ...

Bonus Excerpt
Enjoy!

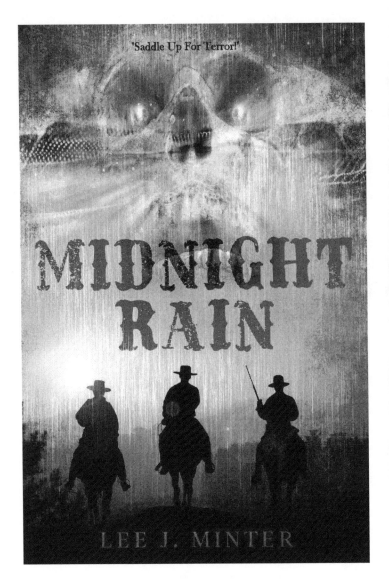

"Saddle Up For Terror!"

MIDNIGHT RAIN

LEE J. MINTER

Midnight Rain

The torrential rainfall had now been coming down for several days as a posse of five bounty hunters with two prisoners rode their horses through the tumultuous weather to get to the town of Red Rock, New Mexico.

They had a bounty to collect of one-thousand dollars a head on the two alleged cattle rustlers and murdering thieves the Chantling brothers, Rickie, and Monroe from El Paso Texas.

The five men in the posse made up of Charley, a rancher and farmer from Arizona, Sanders, a thief himself turned bounty hunter, Peck from Nebraska - a former miner, and Tito, and their leader Eli Boone both ex-soldiers in the Civil War (on the same side of course) and farmers themselves.

All men from different backgrounds but with one thing in common for sure: they were all hardened cowboys and quick and handy with their pistols and had somehow come together to pursue one common interest – bounties.

This posse had been riding their horses for days now with no sign of rest when they stumbled onto a small and desolate town outside of Amarillo Texas that was not on the map a town named Solemn Creek.

Eli looked at the town's welcome sign through a pair of small binoculars he kept in his saddle bag.

"Let's get these horses dry, fed, rested, and some grub in our bellies, and we can start up tomorrow," Eli ordered.

"Sounds like a plan to me. I am tired of riding wet balls in a saddle," replied Sanders, as he pulled back on the reins of his horse to settle him.

"Solemn Creek, what in the wurl kind of name is that for a town?" asked Charley as he spit some of the tobacco he was chewing on the ground.

"Yeah, it ain't that inspirational is it?" Tito stated frowning.

One of the Chantling brothers started laughing that was riding rope saddle and shotgun under the watchful eye of Eli's men.

"What's so damn funny?" Charley asked, eyes narrowing.

"I be damned, I ain't never heard a nigger be so ambidextrous with the white man's language, have you, Ricky?" Monroe said grinning.

"Can't say I have," answer Rickie with a tobacco stain and missing teeth grin.

"You do know what that word ambidextrous mean don't you boy?" Monroe, said, taunting Tito.

Tito rode his horse over to Monroe and put his shotgun underneath the rustler's chin and unsheathed his blade from his scabbard strap around his leg and stuck it in Monroe's gut.

"Blow your cracker brains out while gutting you at

the same time boy?"

Fear formed in Monroe's eyes as he looked into Tito's and seen that this was a man highly capable of doing just what he said he would do and no doubt with little or no remorse.

Monroe broke into a crooked smile.

"Why's I believe you got it, no need for unnecessary violence," he answers back - conceding.

"Well you keep flapping those cracker gums boy, and I am gone blow out your cracker brains, do you understand?" Tito asked.

"Compren'da amigo," Monroe said, still smiling.

"You kill my brother, you're going to have to kill me too boy," Rickie chimed in.

Tito turns around and looks at Rickie.

"Well that was the plan - boy," Tito said bluntly.

The rest of the posse laughed, but Rickie Chantling did not find it all that amusing.

"Fucking bushwhackers," he said, unamused.

"You two are lucky you are two-thousand dollars' worth of dumbness," said Eli to the Chantling brothers.

"Well our Mammy always said we were blessed," answer Monroe, looking over at Tito for a reaction, he got none just a cold dead stare back from him.

"You ain't gone to be such a smart ass when your neck's at the other end of a rope boy," Peck pointed out.

"You know I'll cross that road when I get to it Mister," said Monroe.

"Oh, you're getting to it fast," Eli assured him.

"Boys let's pay Ole' Solemn a visit shall we," Eli said, as they all set mounted on their horses on a ridge staring at the mysterious town below them in the valley.

"Sounds good, like I said, I need to get my sack dry," Sanders grumbled.

"Will you please stop yakking about those wet balls, Sanders," Charley protested.

"Yeah as soon as they get dry," Sanders replied.

Peck chuckled at his compadres antics.

"Hey, you two clowns cut the horse shit and keep your eyes wide-open we still don't know jack rabbit shit about this town we are riding into and why it's not on the map," said Eli wiping the rain out of his eyes.

The two of them nodded apologetically at Eli out of respect.

"Okay let's go," Eli commanded.

Eli and Tito took the lead as they all rode down to the town of Solemn Creek against the sound of the pouring rain and crackling thunder. Their horses' hooves beat the muddy dirt, sloshing through the treacherous terrain, down to a town that was mysteriously not on their map down to a town that was so far at least to them - unknown.

As they rode their horses through the dirt road into Solemn Creek, they could not help but notice how eerily quiet it was on the dirt streets of the town even the Saloon seemed empty which they all knew was uncommon for any town large or small during the weekend.

After all, that was the place where most locals raised hell on a Saturday and were in church on a Sunday to repent for their rousing rebel ways.

"I don't like this Eli, this town is so quiet it might as well be dead," Tito said observantly.

"You might be right about that Tito, but do you smell that stench in the air?" Eli said, with a scowl on his face.

"Like a hot pot of chitlin's," Tito replied.

"Goddamn what they paved this street with horse shit?" said Sanders holding and pinching his nose.

A young man suddenly appeared out of the darkness of teenage years from one of the structures on the dirt street; he was dressed in old worn out clothes with a floppy hat on his head.

"Hey Mister, can I help y'all?" he yelled out to the strangers on horseback as he looked at them with one hand over his eyes to block the rain coming down.

"Yeah, we need to get bunkered down for the night and get these horses fed and out of this weather," said Eli.

"Okay," answers the young man as he continued staring up at them.

A few minutes pass by, and he had said nothing else, he continued staring up at them strangely.

"What's wrong with that boy, is he short a tater or two?" Charley asked.

"Maybe," Sanders replied, as he eyeballed the young men suspiciously.

Eli finally broke the uncomfortable silence between them and the boy.

"So, boy are you going to stand up there and get drenched staring, or are you going to direct us to where we can get a hot meal and a bunk for tonight," he said.

"Sir if I was you…"

"Aiden get those horses in a stable and send them gentlemen over here!" interrupted and commanded a voice in the distance.

"Peck give 'em a hand," ordered Eli.

Eli and his men dismounted from their horses and took what was important to them out of their saddle bags before they made their way over to the voice with prisoners in tow behind them, that had instructed the boy to stable their horses.

The voice had come from the silhouette that Eli had made out standing in front of the doorway of the Saloon and the closer he got, he saw that the silhouette was a pretty young woman in a white dress maybe in her twenties at the most.

"Greetings, y'all the law," she asked, looking at the two men with them bound with rope around their wrists.

"Good evening to you ma'am I guess you could say that, and these two fine fellas got a date with the hangmen's noose in Red Rock, New Mexico, and we gonna make sure they get there promptly."

"Is that a fact," she asked.

"Yep, that's a fact," Eli answered.

"And who do I have the pleasure of conversing with?" Eli inquired.

"My name's Charity and that boy out there is Aiden that took your horses in, but he's a little touch if you get my drift," she said.

Also by the Author

LEE J. MINTER
IN SHEEP'S CLOTHING

LEE J. MINTER
NEVER CRY WOLF

LEE J. MINTER
THE NIGHT TURNER TRIBUNE
Five Tales Of Terror
SAMANTHA JACKSON

LEE J. MINTER
THE NIGHT TURNER TRIBUNE
Five Tales Of Horror + 1
SPELLBOUND

LEE J. MINTER
Twelve Tales Of Horror And Suspense
Dead End

LEE J. MINTER
THEY CALL IT IZZY
A Night Turner Tribune Novella

LEE J. MINTER
ZOMBIE PIMP
A Night Turner Tribune Novella

LEE J. MINTER
THE SPELL
A Night Turner Tribune Novella

Follow me on Twitter **@LJMHorror4u**
or Facebook **LJMHorrorsTales4u**

Follow me on Instagram @ **mintboogie**

Visit me @ my web page at **topcirclepublishing.com**

Made in the USA
Middletown, DE
19 September 2021